Show-and-Tell Surprise

By Jenne Simon

SCHOLASTIC INC.

All rights reserved. Published by Scholastic Inc., *Publishers since 1920.* SCHOLASTIC and associated logos are trademarks and/or registered trademarks of Scholastic Inc.

The publisher does not have any control over and does not assume any responsibility for author or third-party websites or their content.

This book is a work of fiction. Names, characters, places, and incidents are either the product of the author's imagination or are used fictitiously, and any resemblance to actual persons, living or dead, business establishments, events, or locales is entirely coincidental.

ISBN 978-1-338-25619-2

10 9 8 7 6 5 4 3   18 19 20 21 22

Printed in the U.S.A.   40

First printing 2018

Book design by Becky James

The sun rose over the Marvelous Metropolis. Cutie Pie was getting ready for a big day at school. She put something special into her backpack.

It was Show-and-Tell Day!
    Cutie Pie couldn't wait to share her special surprise. And she was not alone. All her friends had something special to show.

"Take your seats," the teacher, Owlette, told the class.

It was not time for show-and-tell yet.

Cutie Pie did not want to wait.
"Psst!" she whispered to Georgia. "What did you bring for show-and-tell?"

Georgia pulled out her fire helmet.

"I wear it when I help fight fires," said Georgia.

"Your helmet shows what a hero you are!" said Cutie Pie.

During story time, Cutie Pie sat next to Kiki.
"What did you bring for show—and—tell?"
Cutie Pie asked.
   "My camera!" purred Kiki. "Isn't it cool?"

Kiki's camera was fancy.
She showed Cutie Pie
some photos she had taken.

"Your camera shows
you are an artist!" said
Cutie Pie.

During music class, Cutie Pie sat next to Violet.

"What did you bring for show-and-tell?" she asked.

Violet pulled out a baton. She was the drum major of the marching band.

Violet led the class in song.

"Your baton shows you are a great leader!" said Cutie Pie.

At recess, Cutie Pie found Duke.
"What did you bring for show-and-tell?" Cutie Pie asked.
"This big dog brought home the gold!" Duke barked.

Duke lifted a trophy over his head.
He had won a big race.
"Your trophy shows how fast you are!"
said Cutie Pie.

The lunch bell rang.
Cutie Pie sat next to Sweetly.
"What did you bring for show–and–tell?" asked Cutie Pie.
"I wrote a song about friendship," Sweetly said.

"Your song shows how sweet you are!" said Cutie Pie.

Cutie Pie smiled, but she was worried. Her friends' stuff was all so special.

What if her surprise wasn't special enough?

Rainbow had a
four-leaf clover.
She was one
lucky poodle!

Dakota's piggy bank
was full.
    She was going to
give her coins to a
good cause.

Squeaker had his passport.
He had raced all over the world!

Now Cutie Pie was in distress.
"Show-and-tell is going to be a mess!" she cried.

Then Cutie Pie had an idea.
Show-and-tell was still a few hours away.
Maybe she could find something new to share.

Cutie Pie got to work in the science lab.
She tried to invent something cool.
But her best was a bust.

Next Cutie Pie drew a map of the park.
A treasure map would be exciting!
But she didn't have any buried treasure.
And a treasure map without a treasure wasn't very special.

Cutie Pie dressed up. She tried to learn some lines from a play.

Then she thought about acting in front of the class.

Cutie Pie shook her head.

She was too shy to perform.

Cutie Pie didn't know what to do.
It was time for show-and-tell.
But she was not a hero or an artist or
a leader.

She did not want to show anything to her class!
Cutie Pie ran out of the room.

"What's wrong?" asked Georgia.
Cutie Pie sniffled.
"All I have for show-and-tell is a pie I made," she said.

"But you baked the pie all by yourself,"
said Kiki.

"I couldn't do that," added Duke.

"How did you make it?" asked Kiki.

"First I mixed the flour, butter, and sugar," Cutie Pie began.

"Then I rolled out the dough. Next I cut the apples and filled the pie. I added secret spices to make it extra tasty."

"That sounds like a lot of work," said Kiki.
"You went to a lot of trouble for us," said Owlette.

"Cutie Pie, your pie is *very* special," said Owlette. "It shows how caring and generous you are!"

"And what a great baker you are," said Violet.

"Now, who wants to eat this special pie?" Owlette asked.

"We do! We do!" the class cheered.

"Last one to the classroom is a Beanie Boo–Boo!" cried Squeaker.

Cutie Pie's sweet treat was the best part of the day.

"Well done, Cutie Pie!" said Owlette.

He gave her a gold star for show-and-tell.

"Your pie deserves a star, too," said Georgia.
But she had a question.
"What's so secret about your spices?"
Cutie Pie smiled. She did not mind sharing.

Cutie Pie used a dash of kindness.
She mixed in a splash of care.
And she added a sprinkle of sweetness.
That was the best way to bake a pie—with love!